How the Dead Count

How the Dead Count

POEMS BY Judith Johnson Sherwin

W·W·NORTON & COMPANY·INC·NEW YORK

A number of these poems have been published by: *The Mississippi Review*, "Sonnet: On Women's Business"; *Black Box #9*, the first North American Audio publication of: "Sonnet: On Women's Business," "The Blob Speaks to Its Mother," "The Alarm," "This Silver Screwdriver," "Plotting the Change of World," "Morning Light," and "Happy Jack Comes Home"; *Some*, "The Blob Speaks to Its Mothers"; *Ante*, "The Toad"; *Nimrod*, "The Old Woman's Song at Passover"; *Counter/Measures*, "Unbelief"; *The Literary Review*, "If I Sing"; *The Minnesota Review*, "The Alarm"; *North American Poetry Network Anthology*, Second North American Audio publication of "The Alarm"; *Salmagundi*, "The Intellectual Pilgrim"; *California Quarterly*, "The Resting Place"; *The Hudson Review*, "Out and In," "Watching the Night," and "The Paradise Avocado"; *The Fiddlehead*, "Three Poses," and "On the Porch of the Travelers' Rest"; *The Midwest Quarterly*, "The Wake for Myself," "Schroedinger's Cat: One," "The Lives of Rain," and "What Priase"; *The New Republic*, "The Imitation of Death"; *The Partisan Review*, "How We Changed;" *Mother Jones*, "Time for Ripeness," and "The Houseguest"; *Connections*, "Highwire"; *The Oyez Review*, "One Day The Doorbell"; *The Falcon*, "Voyager"; *Painted Bride Quarterly*, "Three Power Dances"; *Poetry Now*, "Earths"; *St. Andrews Review*, "How the Dead Count." "The Resting Place" first appeared in *California Quarterly* copyright © 1977 by the Regents of the University of California.

I am grateful to the editors of these magazines. I am most especially grateful to Ron Bayes, editor of *St. Andrews Review*, who published the impossibly long title poem and gave me the *St. Andrews Review* Poetry Prize, 1975. Without the love and support of my husband, Jimmy, my children, Miranda, Alison, and Galen, my parents, Eleanor and Edgar Johnson, and my dear friends, Carolyn Kizer, Carol Bergé, and Naomi Lazard, this book would not have been possible.

Book Design by Antonina Krass,
Typefaces are Janson VIP and Visa.
Manufactured by Vail-Ballou Press, Inc.

Library of Congress Cataloging in Publication Data
Sherwin, Judith Johnson.
How the dead count.
I. Title.
PS3569.H44H6 1978   811'.5'4   77–17473
ISBN   0   393   04485 8   cloth edition
ISBN   0   393   04491 2   paper edition

1 2 3 4 5 6 7 8 9 0

CONTENTS

Part Three: "Sinne of Selfe-Love . . ."

Part Four: The Paradise Avocado

Part Five: From Brussels

Part Six: How The Dead Count

SONNET:

On Women's Business

the Great Emperor, like a snowflake, has laid his head on the line
we walk. i didn't know how not to kick him into the drifts.
don't be boring, the moths whispered, as they unraveled around the
                                                                    flame.
the snow will melt all of us soon enough, especially when these
                                                    november drafts

teach us balance, the snow will flicker around you with greater
                    blankness than mountains of kindness to snow can warm
or tides of consideration of moths can knit together. that small
                                        candle you stem will go white.
we shall go out / together / being boring. listen to that
                                        speaking head swarm
alive out of the snowdrifts. it wobbles. the bees have nested in its
                                                                throat.

there is nothing you can do but make a fool of yourself, like a moth
                                                    under the dead
sea tides. Magna Mater, this is not a popularity poll. there is no way
                                                    you can reverse
the great snowjobs of policy. you are married to policy as to a coil of
                                                    bees in a frozen head
that must sweep you in when they swarm. the tongue flickers, the
                    tongue thickens, that ball wavers, it cannot stay the course

but it wants you, listen to it hum how it wants you, it changes shape,
                    it has risen to become a loaf of bread that chokes the deep
mold-ingrown snowbank gorge of history. you are married to history
                    as to a heavy loaf /
                                        there is no way it will keep.

One

THE BLOB SPEAKS TO ITS MOTHER

just to have held one clear memory of shape.
not always to be approaching some limit other
than can be derived from me. not to be possessed by your voice.
not defined by any voice factored out of my voicelessness.
not to leave remainders of myself each place
i pass over.
        not constantly to find fractions, hardly ingested,
of alien minds worked into my bubbling mass.
not to be forced to race
to feel like an integer
               to get there in one piece.

i swear to you i'd shave away
even my infinitely minute
             variable
                hypothetical
                    disappearing
center for this

and leave myself no more than a function from outside space.

SONG

(after Baudelaire and Creeley)

my voice my silence
my lack of art
my self my science
my hold in the dark

          where everything is clear
          light, calm sensuality

star of breaking and entering, you
who crack light in jet streams
through me, what can i give you

          in a dream of order

lies
       lies
as if all lies were true

LOOKING IN THE MIRROR

                        the eye
that sees the mind

is not
the I that minds.

THE TOAD

i know no certain cure
of ancient ills but new
no calm so clear
as this, to run your nail
along a hardened scar
and draw fresh blood.

take in your hand this toad
(*squat, spattered with sweat,*
sides that puff in and out
bloat, seem to explode
to the touch of your finger, swell
like a bellows, then sink, then fill)

and say: is what you hold
there, working to the goad,
pulse and repulse, my heart
as hearts have worked from the first
day's cold

THE OLD WOMAN'S
SONG AT PASSOVER

so far, so far the stars, so far the stars
so far, so far the stars, the stars so far,
so far, sow far the stars, sow far and far
shofar the stars, the ram's horn will show far
and near, show far what i have come to here.

      my, we are crazy, we are very crazy today
      bitchy, bitchy, rotten bitchy today
      we spit out hard words, we pull them out of our loins
      we unwind long bloody strings of them, look we drip
      thick clotted menstrual blood
      long years past coming, we drip and stink all night
      we take out our teeth and throw them at you, shout
      pray God, pray God they bite.

time is a weavering in us
the shutters in the wall
old blind time a weavering
makes no sense at all

      nasty our age, attacks you, makes you blink
      we vomit up black bile
      our armpits itch, our groin tries to hatch out
      a kind of stringy cheese no use to anyone
      come near and dip your fingers, bless us, bless the old
      the useless clefts of loins, the soiled fold

so far the stars, sow far and far the stars
suffer the stars, suffer the stars so far
as they will come, suffer the little, the great
and the mad black stars that blow out heaven's gate

      the night rises in us, swells up a thick sourdough
      we'd like to break you open with long life and night.
      the night puffs our bellies with gas, we've been leavened so long

it breaks through the heartskins, cracks open the loaf that tries
to raise you with it, the voice of the leaf, the whistling trees

cold stars, black stars that blow out heaven's gate
far holes of heaven
                    and we so far to them
so far suffer, no closer let them come
lest we blow out heaven's gate and God fall dumb

and burst before we're dead.

UNBELIEF

twisted in wood, i saw
the mouth bud to a smile
turning in blood, i knew
the eyes gape to a hole

and there, where rivers run
through reddening caves of light
shot to a beam, and torn
by love, the threads fall mute

and from the arms pulled tall
on the long cross i taste
the nerveless hands bleed pale
the bones part in the wrist

drawn from the thin-gummed smile
the cheeks melt down like glass
say of Him what you will
your will dissolves with His

IF I SING

for Senator Robert Kennedy
and the Rev. Martin Luther King, Jr.

the blood, that's nothing. whistle my blood
into tracks you follow, you're all
you were, not less, not more. holler
my heart under your skin, i'll still be cold.

when we transplant the will
we'll have done something. think
spilt those strong minds for change
            and in some quiet men
their rage to do hammering still.

nothing's wasted. i could believe
earth's proud bodies held
if one chamber thundered under my skull
how those loud dead live.

ODE TO THE MOTHER AS BANKER

I

wind up the child, make him go
onto that floor where money will burn for him
under a roof of gold /
                              tell him to keep himself
sweet for such uses as wise men know
when every ceiling falls
and the heart given out at interest is carried over
teach him to raise his hands, to lower his hands

wind up the child, he is our stock exchange
in him we call our talents in
                              and put them out to grow
teach him to buzz in circles, he is the gold
flame round whom all currencies float
from whom all issues rise

wind him up, make him bend and stoop
he is a tattered elephant /
                              all wrinkles and grey hide
his hands are ledgers apt to hold
not put and call alone, but fall and rise
make him balance the legends that leap to his count
total the centuries in his eyes

good saint, let him study not to see
how love's cold artifact in your mind
last year made sun and mountains rise
and all our humane glory thrust
out of the crumpled green of his skin
the coppery alloy of his fingers' ends

i am winding the child up, i have taught him to crawl
under that dome where angels plunge
in flaming dividends and fall
i am letting him go with the golden moths of the sun
his teeth are sliding into the cash drawer
his paunch scurries back and forth with the weights of the clock
his fingers twist with the worms under heaven's dress
where they twitch the sound coin out and assay the weight

his heart has studied what he can see and hear
and, at one with all honest brokers, know
see the great chain of being chain his vault shut
see the natural orders flow in his cash flow
of days /
            he has borrowed against the milky way,
holds the blind craters of the moon in trust

he is running through the sea sand and every grain rings
in that haven where death rings sweet and free /
                                    such wise metal is he
                                            grown
he is tearing himself apart where every mote flies
and gilds my hair, he is dancing into the sun
with the summer flies /
                    while his paradise measuring heart
kicks out a quick tick tock.

THE BREAKFAST AND
DINNER NEWS FLAMENCO

your feet are wavering but the night is miked
out of which we stalk each other. if you want to hear,
listen to the switchblades whistle. each leaf
as it falls will slice the air so thin you can bite

it off with your toast for breakfast. if you want to hear,
the air will pick up the least click of your life
being spilled with the tea and the toasted news you can bite,
next morning's eye-opener, true to the nearest squeal

of fear and dismay. the last click of your life
will go out on the airwaves to that great river of eels
in America i see catching your nearest squeal,
live, on four channels. don't cry, for the world's night

will be yours, and you'll die of it. great rivers of eels
will coil fear and dismay as they wait to hear you dine
on your life sliced thin. don't cry for the world's night;
for it picks up the last poor clatterings, toes and teeth,

and sprinkles them out like salt. we shall see you and dine
on the switchblades, the castanet panic, the floor miked to hear
how you stamp the world's night clean out of you, toes to teeth.
i want you to stamp very hard. please stamp twice.

THE ALARM

for Henry Kissinger

the hands lie low,
slow but busy, they circle
around, they juggle
with numbers, they add scores
up, all day we are
the scores they add. without us
to back them those figures have
nothing to tell. the face
stays blank.

poor face, by day a dull
pasty patience, by night a moon-
struck gleam by the side of the bed just
back of the world's left ear, only noticed
to measure a universe beside
itself. it blinks, whirs.

it would give anything, millions
of minute advantage for the good
old days its masters ticked off, barter
both hands and its glow-in-the-dark
pale waiting if it could get
the reins in its hands once more
subject to nothing, with every face a wheel
to drive down our days, life's charioteer
as it used to be
          instead of this endless circling
for nothing
          at a distance.

it would throw out
gardens of digital eyes if it could just once
get those two hands (and the arms' weight behind them) on

a scythe it could chop
us down with.

it is not as smart
as it thinks it is. its head
has nothing but springs inside though
springs have their points.
its face dilates, swells, spirals in
and out like a nebula. the mind
behind the face is buzzing
gases: no swords converts
to ploughshares but tightcoiled springs
straightens to spears and curved space
flattens to charts.

                    even now
it throws out a hundred feeling
wheels for each numbered stop
of your heart, ticktock, it is armed
for war, it will get
us all, it jumps up to ride
your back, it will carry away
your office safe, it's running like mad up
the heavens not down, it will go
berserk/off/bong, programmed to stop
your heart to make
all systems go

                    count
down how even the choicest mind's
vehicle shooting its springs
out can run amok
behave like bomb not clock
if the heart be not
set right.

THE INTELLECTUAL PILGRIM

A Parable

". . . but only for God's first creature, which was light:
to have light, I say, of the growth of all parts of the world."

—SIR FRANCIS BACON, *The New Atlantis*

"He who the sword of Heaven will bear
should be as holy as severe."

—WILLIAM SHAKESPEARE, *Measure for Measure*

it raged by day and raged by night
they had to cancel every flight
and after waiting through the rain
i thought: *no sin to take a train.*
yes, Lord, no merit sure to stand
in transit to the Holy Land.
we parted glad in sleep to pass
from Egypt through the Wilderness,
to cover all that crawling way
of forty years in half a day.

along the aisle on my right hand
i saw God's Special Forces stand
unloaded from the Angels' fleets
one jot too late to capture seats.
their medals burnished, brushed their suits /
a troop of Heaven's parachutes /
Michael had led them gallantly
between the Devil and the sea
that their rough hands might serve again
to beat back Satan's breath from man.

Lord, but a bridge of hearts outspanned
to see your armies close at hand
the train slid over rails of bone
skulls packed the chasms stone by stone
long cantilevers stretched their grace
of wills broken and bent in place
while human torches flamed at night

to be our vision and our light /
bones white as tracks sparked, blazed, and said
our lives took fire from these live dead.

what grinning face, what withered hand
bid welcome to the Holy Land
these legions dropped from Paradise
with hand of fire, heart of ice—
now, out of sight stayed out of mind
we left those lanterns far behind
God's Great Society our dream
we saved our tears for Jordan stream
night was forgotten, day began /
sure, greater wisdom hath no man.

friend, heart, i could not think of rest
tears were a slackening at best
he that in truth would win his wings
must guard his heart from human things
must blot out pity, blot out pain
crack down on giving and on gain
demolish both desire and fear
utterly root out love. austere
and clear the mind casts out its lead.
the end is all / the way is dead.

i thought: *no loss to go by train*
the way that measured endless pain
to those before me. i can say:
no merit in the harder way
no excellence, but burning pride
in those who must be crucified /
the iron mean, the primitive
mean clash of an iron way to live,
rise up in anguish, fall in rage
die, falter, let melt the golden age.

yes, Lord, my Savior, i can tell:
we that cared / not for Heaven or Hell,

we came where wilder souls had passed
and saw Jerusalem at last
and found what we had known was true,
nothing there altered, nothing new /
we entered, who had come for truth,
and bore unflinching all their ruth
whose withered hand and flaming face
bore witness they had come for grace
and all we saw or loved was light
to make that balance come out right.

THE RESTING PLACE

WEST VIRGINIA SLAG SLIDE

where the earth lies i dig
up truth by accident, then throw it away
with the summer thunder.
the town weathers a quiet face
to our clatter. no fuss, please.
outside the mine a slag heap
rages. what i don't need gets big,
won't hold back weight or water,
when the earth moves can't stay
quiet, trustworthy, won't state
any meaning for peace. loud,
the pile argues, shifts its weight,
slips, thicker than blood,
just once when the town's asleep
then rests its case.
a thousand lives go under.
truth lies on their mouths
a heavy, metallic mud.
no digging out.

Two

THIS SILVER SCREWDRIVER

love came to me with transistors in his hair
and one antenna up
the tubes of a crackling static under his empty
eyes, and laughed as he snapped his fingers and gave
some dude the beat:

listen to the summer rumble
open yourself up along the breastbone
with this silver screwdriver, peel the skin
back, chisel the ribs away and hold them open
with the point of this silver screwdriver, make yourself say:

i shall be dull as clay, heavy as clay
soft, forming myself to every impression, gentle, grateful to the hand
as muddy clay in a river bed. i shall die
as love wills, i shall harden and crackle with the stars
with the point of this silver screwdriver
but i shall not dream of anything as unforgiving
as this summer night that lies on my belly like thunder.

WHAT THE HOUSE OFFERS

sweet, when you're lazy
safe in your locked
efficiency

(life is not a circus
we will have no circuses)

        don't forget
as the toothed wheels mesh
and the door swings out

i will leap the tall vault
that domes back of your ear
where the audience waits
where the eyes are strung
in a glitter of lights

i will dance the steel nets
as they float high over
the pit of your eye
where the wires run

i will hoot and shout
flash from height to height
the applause will ring out
the alarm sound
something will snap

the charged net will hum
you will laugh and cry
at the end of play
where the stars / break
their tides of light
you will not know why

and the great waves come

and the house will not say

WHAT PRAISE

when you are old, my dear, what shall you praise?
steady in judgment, balanced, grown most wise
with letting go, you shall count what you still prize.
not God, Who set Time carver to your days,
giving you life in slices, light in rays,
set Space watchdog, let no one steal past his eyes
and fill all cubes at once, not Love whose size
was a cage to tell your joys out, a safe / what praise?

why, this praise, this: praise life, that having been such
as you have known it, was not ever too much
to count and cancel, rough, was not so rough
it could rub you away, muddy, spotted, could not smutch
your palm, in what it gave you gave enough.
nothing within your reach was hard to touch.

TIME EATEN UP, DAY GONE

omelette

                              diningroom
              we were red and white
striped fish and under the stars that spelled out ciaou
that night we sang out to old man river,
one easy over, don't you wash me out
tonight, hashed brown, if you love me, don't
in your logrolling short order frenzy roll
me into that hot salt
sunny side up / gulf you go for down there

well the mackerel in the sea, he
guessed i was greased and rarin' to go, the laily
worm with her gold comb
knew but wouldn't say how long
gone soon / the magic splashed crackling to break of day

and all the fresh fried out of us
the sizzle cooled down and the log
jam spewed into the gulf
that streams the sun down hoe
down shake it down drop it down fall down call down
the river down lie down low down slow
down go   /   down   /   forever

TURNING TO YOU

after my heart had sizzled and turned
over for you, you took it off the heat
laid back the skin freckled
cover, which had burned
picked out the white meat

i wish i could say this was the last
time love had lit me
this heart that had three times over
turned on a spit / never lost its ginger
swore never to lie in any man's hand
again like a toad alive /
                              still turned chicken

still brought its heat to you
brought the crisp skin inviting teeth
brought the good use, the crackle
the rush / the swelling juice
of its deep
              venomous
                        sweet
                              and soon
turned meat.

THE FABULOUS TEAMSTERS

up from West 86 St., banging, against all hope
dark sun, dark sun
                      the buzzing of small rain
nyah nyah, and i outside
not here but fourteen floors down
in the beeping of trucks right onto your windowpane

well, i couldn't go forward, all roads blocked off and worse
midnights of tubes tied
all over this midnight town
so i stripped my gears with a roar into reverse

backed two Allied trailers up your wall / sunshine
if my tailgate falls /
with the shock / off, and this heavy vanload tries
of uninsured housewares to bump clatter up the wall,
what you find that falls

up should be no surprise.
reach, please and now, for the ground, happy love, take hold
of no matter all that flies.

we are too full of eyes
see too much to see each other. we have sold
past taking what's out of the brownout sent to us
truck up the bricks after truck
load not signed for, our lives, too, sent back after a fuss
or just not seen, dark sun.

                            buoyant, i for you, you for me,
by levity pulled up
in our boisterous negative momentum, honestly,
gently, ridiculously, praise God, let's be

love's teamsters who have found
if you're not sent up you never get off the ground.

OUT AND IN

quick fish, flickering fish
you blink of the world's eye
when will you move
easily in me
no crazy flapping
on a hook in the heart
but smooth
a seam drawn alive
under the lake's skin

THE SIDES

you offered me a choice: the white pawn or the black.
i took the black and at once you moved
today you're in Mexico on the other side of the chessboard
busy with counters / tomorrow
you'll be on the whiteside of a new
gambit in Amsterdam / next week on the gold
side of an oil stockpile in Egypt / but today
the inventory rides high
today you've taken stock of your center
and you see that it will hold. today you see
that you can gain a minute advantage on the kingside
by going to London immediately. i've offered a pawn
but it isn't enough to keep you. maybe you suspect
that it's poisoned. merely by flying to Africa
for a weekend you can transform the whole position.

oh my enemy whom i love and must play each day
the market falls / come back
from as far as you've gone into the basic endgames
from so far there is no distance
from inside the iguana's eyelids
from the green stone monument to the dead auk
from the farside of my tap tapping left shoe
from the mucous membrane of last night's repeated checks
from the most remote corner of God's mouth
from inside the toenails of your right foot
from the gold moon gong of the white king's belly
from the huge brass bowl
of these mountains' sacrifice into which you have crawled
while the sun licks your ears like a shaggy fat chow
you would shake off if you could

the sides are chosen /
                    you have nowhere else to go.

PLOTTING THE CHANGE OF WORLD

from sweet and stern sleep, carelessly waking
the tidal currents awash out of the stars
called me where one dead comet fell
its tail unlit. late night. i heard a machine,
late late yestreen, and i heard the new moon hum
that had no halo. i sat up, leaned on one
elbow. though my late eyes lay
closed i saw the machine sway, sweet and stern
and late, its tail unlit, and polished shining
steel mirrored, shaped something like a dentist's x-ray
machine machine that calls the child from home
and the tidal currents awash out of the stars
close by your cheek and humming you asleep
machine that late i saw
hover low even over you, hover low
over you. low, you lay asleep and did not see. my eyes
machine machine that pulls the eyes from home
and lets all dreaming nations lay down their steel
teeth my eyes fast closed i did not sleep i saw

how dreadfully love's world had changed in you
since you had hummed and called
me where one comet fell since you had been
called to sleep and called not to lean
on one elbow, since your late eyes lay
closed, did not turn to me, did not turn, never turned, since late
since late the machine
of sweet stern sleep had with no halo hummed
over our sleeping world its tail unlit
not more shining than it was mirrored steel
not more moon than it was comet tail
unlit, oh not more late than it was hovering

close by your cheek like love shaped something like a dentist's x-ray
machine from sweet and stern sleep carelessly waking

i had wanted to be love's poet and had failed
dreadfully as love's world had changed in me
and now i saw machine that calls the heartbeat
up from its haven and tunes the comet's tail
machine machine that sings
your late late yestreen eyes
most generously asleep how little love's poet
was needed to bear the night away how the late comet will
sow nations' teeth in the wind and the tidal wash
sternly asleep and you not rise
and i not rise with you
to hover over one another's sleeping
close by your cheek and eyes shaped something like
machine that is not needed to call your mind
when it has need of sleep when nothing is lost
nothing is lost i say.

i woke my eyes fast closed and there i saw
machine of stern and careless sleep that brings
the change of world awake work silver the dear
tides of your eyes most generously asleep
work silver on
your hallowed sail-
tossed comet cheek that rains the haloed world
away machine that calls the heartbeat up
close by to where comets rain down their steel
not more shining than it was mirrored sail
oh not more moon than it was comet tail
and tail well lit

           alone in the world *the change
of world, the change that bears the world away*
generosity of spirit does not fail.

Three

"Sinne of Selfe-Love ..."

"Sinne of selfe-love possesseth al mine eie,
And al my soule, and al my every part;
And for this sinne there is no remedie,
It is so grounded inward in my heart."
—Shakespeare

SCHROEDINGER'S CAT: ONE

turned his back
on the cat
in the mirror. his eyes,
not made like mine, saw
no shadow he knew there,
no sign of a cat on the floor.

as if he'd stepped in dirt
he shook out a hind paw.
the room shrank to a point
on a vanishing line
then filled out once more.

alone in the room, the only cat
in the world (which also took
up none of his space)
he leaped to fill the patch
of sun stretched out
on a chair.

on his notched fur the sun
sharpened its claws, then slept.
the room, through a hole in a screen,
bombarded him with fire.

i have been in that sweat
box, scientist of myself,
a lifetime or more
and met nothing i'd wake for.

i watch the motes drill my box.
in this world, the cat takes fire
in himself, in the other he burns
on his chair.

THE GOOD TECHNICIAN

I am making a shape in space and I refuse,
however I heft its mass or measure the press
of its parts in action or rest, to consider its use.

how the armature will stand up to my dense abuse
of function, its form as skeleton fail to compress!
I am making a shape in space and I refuse

to lighten its load or allow it to make an excuse
if its joints unhinge under friction or duress
of its parts in action or rest. consider its use:

a balance of forces I measure, a frame I induce
to stand when the forces I force to coalesce
with their charges build shapes in space and cannot refuse

to force from them space you can dance in, space that can choose
to dance. on a turning stage would your feet caress
some part in action or rest? to consider your use

is no part of my form or function, or yours. we reduce
our choice when we choose to measure less than the stress.
I am making a shape in space and I refuse,
with these parts in action or rest, to consider the use.

SCHROEDINGER'S CAT: TWO

A QUANTUM DEMONSTRATION

set-up
there was a box with a screen with a hole.
there was a place for a cat to sit.
there was a nice little syringe with a needle attached.
when the needle touched the cat the cat could not move.
there was a box with a screen with a hole.

1 THE CAT WAS THERE / 2 THE CAT WAS NOT THERE
1A nothing happened 1B something happened
2A nothing happened 2B something
happened

1A1 the cat was still there   2A1 the cat was not there
  1A2 the cat was not there   2A2 the cat appeared
    1B1 the cat was hurt   2B1 the cat was there
      1B2 the cat was not hurt   2B2 something else happened

1A1A the cat was hurt
1A1B the cat was still there
1A2A the cat disappeared
1A2B the cat died
            1B1A the cat died
            1B1B the cat did not die
            1B2A the cat was hurt later
            1B2B the cat was still not hurt
                    2A1A the cat was still not there
                    2A1B the cat appeared
                    2A2A the cat was hurt
                    2A2B the cat was still not hurt
                            2B1A the cat was hurt
                            2B1B the cat was not hurt
                            2B2A nothing else happened
                            2B2B something else
                                    happened
1A1A1 the cat was bombarded with radioactive particles
1A1A2 the cat was bombarded with something else which was nasty
1A1B1 the cat was bombarded with radioactive particles
1A1B2 the cat disappeared
1A1B3 the cat did not disappear
1A2A1 the cat came back

49

1A2A2 the cat did not come back
1A2B1 something else happened
1A2B2 Schroedinger got a new cat
      1B1A1 something else happened
      1B1A2 Schroedinger got a new cat
      1B1B1 the cat was bombarded with radioactive particles
      1B1B2 the cat was bombarded with something very nasty
                                    indeed

      1B2A1 the cat died
      1B2A2 the cat did not die
      1B2B1 the cat was still not hurt
      1B2B2 the cat was very hurt indeed
            2A1A1 the cat was still not there
            2A1A2 the cat appeared
            2A1B1 nothing else happened
            2A1B2 something else happened
            2A2A1 the cat died
            2A2A2 the cat did not die
            2A2B1 the cat was bombarded with
                        radioactive particles
            2A2B2 the cat was bombarded with the
                    nastiest little particles in the lab
              2B1A1 the cat died
              2B1A2 the cat did not die
              2B1B1 nothing else happened
              2B1B2 the cat was bombarded
                        like mad
              2B2A1 Schroedinger bought a
                        new cat
              2B2A2 the cat was bombarded
                        with shit
              2B2B1 the cat died
              2B2B2 the cat was very very
                        hurt indeed

IF YOU THINK
    THE QUESTION IS
        WHY ARE THERE THESE
            VARIATIONS IN RESULT

GO BACK TO THE BEGINNING
    AND JOIN
            SCHROEDINGER'S CAT

WHY DID SCHROEDINGER POSIT A CAT FOR THIS
DEMONSTRATION?

THREE POSES

One: Before a Mirror

i know your eyes
sometimes i have pushed aside the lids
diving, swum through to the skies
widening irises of alien blue.
i know your lips have known
how lips may shape and frame
the sounds of words and meanings i must own
as mine and yet disown. i know your voice
empty as any framed sound where it grows
behind the throat, rounds the tight chords
in emptiness, tides through the teeth
without my thought or single choice. i say i know your mind
the will that acts and forces while i watch
fingers, flex, reflex, ripples, jointed bars
to hold me part of you. i cannot find
you in these opening circles for i strike
through them to shatter you.

Two: Before a Marble Pan

your hooves hammer a dance
that cuts the air up. where they yank you
your body follows, whipping in the wind.
as your spiked head jerks back
on your neck like a mace on its chain, slaps out that barbed
steel mass of hooks, your hair, to tear at the light
and as your arms snap out
do you never fight the whip that makes you crack?
you should rebel, your will against its whirl.
have you no cunning to still, no force to subdue
that rattling dance? or is the heart that throws you
half heart of the beast and half man's heart in you?
if you could see your face
you would detest that blood which makes you shake
pulse to its rhythm, fall along its flow.

yet this line follows smooth. it will not break,
bends free your hands, folds arms and shoulders back
to hold you open where the still winds blow.
so sudden this catch of the breath, these pipes in the reeds.
played by this music you receive and know
the beast in single rhythm with the man.

Three: Before a Mirror

you reach out too
to smooth the broken ripples of this glass.
we stroke the lids aside, swim their crested floods
to meet and cut our reaching hands on ice.
i have come to know:
we cannot touch on any outward flow
of mind to music. we must turn our eyes
to inward blackness, back to back, and act
in outward unison, divorced in fact.
beyond rest or caesura, whole, i know
seen by no alien eyes my eyes will find
closed in and walled around
in their own caves sensed mirrors of the mind,
blood's image on the brain outlined in nerves
that flash in their circuits. cleared from the source unknown
by the heart's action hewn out of the bone
two selves will move one pulse, one inside one.

THE DISSOLUTION

A PARABLE

late, late dawn, when i carved myself a tomb
of one rough block of stone
encrusted well with vines
and moss that i stripped off to free the line,
then scraped the rockwall clean

though i left one face wild, one face alone
entangled still in green
glowering
        the roof sloped down, smooth stone
for me to fall upon
lost in my mortal creature's death, to mourn
beat, beat the bones that i had walked upon
and leave no sign
though my tears fell on just one spot alone

no hollowed cup might come
no smallest indentation in the tomb
no pock, no pit, no softening / stone /
                    firm

and on the side where vines
and moss crawled still, the flowers came to twine
color and stem, to climb
in hot profusion, and the bees to hum

such luxury of passion i made come
your fertile earth grew rich upon my pain
your hunger was my own
your thirst the very thirst i suffered from
a world to fill my grief and not lie dumb

in that black soil your worms
braided, too ripe content to come
into my darkened home

54

to feed on what was mine
jungles sprang up to worship your cruel sun
which nourished them with pain
through my fierce constant nourishment of rain
nothing was left undone
to keep all safe within
that room, so what was mine would mine remain
not crumble, no, nor burn
in agony of lime,
not feed the hunger of the flowering worm
of silences, not turn
to rotten use which falls to fill the loam.

so, as that jungle grew it hid the tomb
the roof which had been clean
of moss and vine lay foul, damp, overgrown
while rotting flowers rotted through the stone
my tears could not defame
their roots augers of flame
that burnt fresh holes to let the foulness in

through one of those holes i came
into my narrow room
where all i loved lay fragrantly alone,
and found the self was gone

purely consumed, no trace left that had been
my passion and my own
laid with such care to dream
in peace, to sleep in fragrances of steam

my love had killed it
                        luxury of the eye
dissolved the soul but left the carcase dry.

THE WAKE FOR MYSELF

now in the night i wake and watchful keep
what vigil and remembrance still may keep
here, mine, the love which i alone must keep

so long i must mourn, not the stone the stone
heart it wants more mourns than i locked alone
in separation from the thing i own

still might i keep fast locked, boxed in my hands
still castled, dungeoned rightly in my hands
what from the first was given to my hands

but that my love some conscious waking knew /
that itch of hunger, deepening, burrowed, grew,
dissolved what flesh and walls once held it true

now soul, my soul, you lie so long apart
an entity, what was so long a part
and still i must retake you part by part

i search you with my study, and you fade,
whimper, renege, rage, weaken, and evade,
and still i cry what cry this severance made:

why soul, my dear, whom would you rage withal
whom would you grace with passion, brand withal
whom comfort, dear, whom murmur love withal?

still must i hate who bored my body free
to rage both worlds / in a heartbeat severed me /
you comfort whom i suffer constantly.

THE IMITATION OF DEATH

tell me, dear mindmate, what you see in me
to knot your eyes to the same beam as my eyes,
hold me as your target, fasten my sight your prize,
so rivet me, to the death, in what you see?
why, you can see nothing more. blind but for me /
i am your world, your vision, and devise
except for your sight of me your seeing dies.
so in my life your life is what you see.
and when i lie you lie, when i wake to rise
i walk imprisoned through tunnels of your eyes
to see myself live through your sight of me.
and when, in this glass, this glass corpse crucifies,
wrists shattered, pierced by nails that are your eyes,
i shall know, not that i feel, but that you see.

how easy to tell you, mindmate, even He
i heard died in earnest on His cross, heard chose
to know the deep bones break open, the ribcage disclose /
crown of the night / how the heart dies on its tree /
i promise you now, in that icon of dying, He
saw no way to shake off this icon of sight, but rose
possessed by that self, carved in blood, weathered in those
Who died to hang their hearts from His heart's tree.
what shall i bring back out of my tunneled repose,
weighted with earthen death? shall i wake what rose
icon, fable, mined in blood from the sap of the tree?
i know no Passion. if this grinding down disclose,
eclipsed / crown of the night / as the sun's edge shows
round its night heart, one tongue of flame, i might swing free.

THE ONE WHO MEANS TO COME BACK

i am going deeper into the earth
which wants me to. the tunnels that lead me down
count each feeling clod
that stops my mouth, such a weight of passage is on me.
the cars that gather my journey
        tumbrils scarred with graffiti
        from the other world, the mark of their warlords on them,
shake rattle and roll against the way
they must take me. today, today
they carry my mind. tomorrow they'll take my blood away.

how empty these cups, the wardead
i cannot wake, no mass
to open, to close in my wake /
i drop through their eyes like a plumb line.

there is a fate that speaks in me
bearded like that mean, dirty prophet
who hunched on the last low step
before the sun let me be sucked down in
where what i cannot do
is alone worth doing well.

such fury i bring with me
as would lead these dead to thunder
and make them drink their death like rain / water.

Four

The Paradise Avocado

HOW WE CHANGED

A PROSE SESTINA

i didn't move. what else? another day. i thought of you. the iceberg.
i was here.

i was here. i didn't move the iceberg. what else? i thought of you
another day.

another day i was here. i thought of you. i didn't move. what else:
the iceberg.

the iceberg, another day. what else: i was here. i didn't move. i
thought of you.

i thought of you, the iceberg. i didn't move another day. i was here,
what else?

what else: i thought of you. i was here, the iceberg. another day i
didn't move.

move, what else? day: thought of you. the iceberg was here.

ANOTHER STORY

A PROSE VILLANELLE

i saw a tree. i couldn't find you. you were going to eat me.

the refrigerator looked empty. i didn't know what to do. i looked out at the tree.

you looked hungry. i thought we were through but now you wanted to eat me.

it wasn't easy to do. i looked at the tree.

we moved up so slowly. halfway through, you got me.

if i could have pulled free i could have saved you. i was almost up the tree when you ate me.

THREE SHORT CHEERS

A BLUES

1.

one led to five which led to three which led to four. you left your hat
in the freezer and your teeth on the floor.
i didn't see you anymore.

2.

two led to seven which led to nine which led to five. when the pig
keeps turning around the mushrooms may not arrive.
you said in your letter it was good to be alive.

3.

morning led to doormat which led to tomcat which led to two. that
didn't leave us with much of anything we could do.
if i could string anymore together i'd send a basket to you.

THE PARADISE AVOCADO

A TALKING BLUES

She was growing and growing. Every branch had to take a long time. Every leaf took a few weeks to lose its shine. She had been doing it a long time. Every day had to put out a new stem to lose its shine. She had been trying and trying. Sometimes she didn't know how to take a long time. Every year she knew less of how to lose her shine. The newness rubbed off and then had to be put back on. She had found that powder worked best because it took away the shine. A special kind of green dust would make the glow of youth not last too long. The polished side of each leaf had a tendency to stay so long. People would ask her why are you staying so long and she would say because the party hasn't lost its shine.

She had been staying and staying. She had been doing it till she turned green. Nobody bothered to stop and ask her why are your leaves so long and green. She thought it had something to do with the moisture of the ground she was standing on. The ground she was set in was one which held and held its drink. People would stop and ask and ask her why are you falling around and drooping down. She would say maybe it's because I don't seem to be turning brown. If she could learn how to turn brown too soon she would not have to stay green so long. The ground she was set in was one that made your every root sink.

It was a deadly kind of job to be greening and greening as she stayed. She thought it had something to do with the increasing thickness of her stem. The children sometimes would stop and ask her why is your stem getting so grossly thick. She told them that maybe it had to do with how many things there were to soak up. The shoes and watering cans were all over the floor and the socks would definitely have to be mopped up. She was bending and bending but her stem went right on picking everyone up. Her husband thought maybe it had something to do with her increasing refusal to soak things up. Sometimes when she was feeling green she had a tendency to think she had had enough. Her children wanted to know whether she hadn't been with them more than long enough.

She was always doing and doing but her leaves were beginning to get too dry. She thought maybe it had something to do with the rate of drainage of her clay pot. The sun was always shining and that tended to make things hot. She was always gathering drinks in May but the drainage continued at a constant rate. Her husband wanted to know why her leaves were sweeping the ashes out of the flue. She thought maybe it had to do with a feeling of being rootbound in that pot. He thought that maybe it had to do with her not having enough to do. A green young thing needs room to grow even in a chimney, she said, even when it's the household mascot it needs a new room for its pot.

Something was growing and growing inside her left leafy stem. It grew and grew until it felt unpleasantly hard under his hand. It grew until she suspected that maybe it might turn out to be a friend. Maybe it should be checked out she suggested but he said the pull of the drainage was all in her mind. Something began to grow and grow and it didn't act like a leafy stem. It pulled and pulled until she suspected that maybe it was the roots and vines of children without end. Maybe it better be pruned they decided and her children didn't ask her when. I am growing a little something she said and I hate to cut it off before its time. Never mind, her husband watered her every night, you just haven't lost that leafy shine.

They pruned away her sweetest leaves because they were blocking off the chimney of everybody's sun. You can't stand in the way like that they complained, it's time to let the fresh air in. She had lost her roundest fruit but they couldn't prune away the thick stem. It's time to winter my withers and lay low, she creaked, before I stand in everybody's sweet sun. You just relax said the waterers and we'll clear you off the line. She was growing and growing but the end of growth took a long long time. Tomorrow I'll learn how to stop she said. He said tomorrow you'll be just fine.

Five

From Brussels

WATCHING THE NIGHT

lately
it has seemed to me
                the full moon round
                and feathered like an owl
as if i'll never live
to be   hunched over
a fat old woman
in a tree
                to fill the branches
under me   with plucked out down
and dust   remains of small
whistlebone

                animals

how i'd hone   that moon down
while i'd puff up   crescent
        slip
and whistle and
          call and
          holler and
              hoot the
cold oak hollow   of lust
faithfully   the whole night full
until i bust.

MY PRIDE

i sat in a well made box, pleased
to call the space i found
there mine, and it seemed more
than i needed at the time. you
came with a word and a frown
abstracted, uneasy, knocked
the catch crooked.

                       so i crept
into a roomier box, walls
at angles i didn't expect,
allowing a crazy growth no
one taught me how to name.

to exert a claim is
fearful, difficult.
what force i could bring to bear
or what exact, i
guess but hold back
not to spare you, no

but because you can't refuse
what i don't ask.

DEAD MIND

cold territory, tough
comfort: under
a hunting moon, what freehold

always now
masked man
when you crawl into my head
face averted, not looking at me

the hinges
creak, those bones that joined
when i edged out of my mother
crack
to make room.

i welcome
the unmistakable signals
of health. heart gallops
loud hoofbeats after so many years /
breath scurries to fire
what would be words if you got
within reach. see the smoke leap up
in clots over the rooftops,
giving the high sign.

if you shoot
the lock off, break down
the door, i may scald the skin
off you, leave you useless

as i don't now
so gentle am i for you
when i let you in

bandito, dance in my head

in your high-heeled boots, tell me
why must i
shower you most with lust
when we're not in bed?

TIME FOR RIPENESS

when i talk to you
the plums burst open, half
eaten by yellow jackets,
drip purple juice down
that sticks to my hands. yellow velvet
droplets with legs spill
out of the fruit, crawl
over my hands, lick the syrup.

i say here what i can't say
to you. when i try
to move you, i have no sure touch
i'm stung. each word i say
i think of the heavy work
i make of you, not of you
or of what you make of this

which gives you nothing of me.
no purity / in thought
or action.

take the honey out of the hive, smear
the delicate, hairy legs, the striped
bellies, the crisp
shells with their own juices, come devour
the furred flower
of bitterness.

THE YELLOW JACKETS

they're dying, they crawl
into the house to die
in the breadbox, on the floor
where i don't always see them, walk on them, feel them crunch.

to ask something of you scares my
guts out, makes them drop
down whining and crawl away. you'd
feel forced to answer. here's
a dead thing on my plate
trapped in what i was going to eat, pulled
by greed /

                    if you said
                    please come back to life
                    i might take that risk
                    now and for years full
                    of you

             stopped cold
death where he thought was food
                    who can't take it
                    all the way
                    to you, say i'll make you
                    live again too

            curled
on his side, legs curled
over his belly, sting
twitching

SHOW-OFF

a cold wind blows
out of my head to you, lifts
your hair, breathes fast,
urgent, ridiculous
in your ear, on your throat. look
what a clown i am, what a lummox, i'm blowing you over,
i'm wrecking the city for you, the mayor will call
a disaster / hear what i won't
tell you across the clogged
shells of city and silence we've chosen
our metier.

so far i find you here
other end of nowhere. i'm far too
hoping i can't hurt you
in what i don't force from you   /   my windy city
who live too far from the bone

i think forcing is what
you need, and i hurt you most
when i let myself die down, don't press too hard,
don't bite into the bone, don't make you shudder.

both of us too
decent   /   for all our bluster.

MAKING FICTIONS

an art
i know. holy cow, i've been
sky-jacked for twenty years now
the aisles ass high
with dead children, people like bombs
dropping all sides of me, splashing
while i play
the heroine, battle
to get free, no scarecrow
stiff-limbed chessplaying hero
who won't even dance in the aisles without
keeping his dignity
is going to get off with me.

so i bring the plane down
what's left of it, in my own
free desert, everyone dead,
husbands, wives, children, eaten by laughing
hyenas, or run off under the hasty
sun, or ransomed, why not,
somehow, happy. i've saved
everyone's life by killing
everyone /
        and you meet me
at the oasis
with a bouquet.

REVENANT

today
they're ringing the bells on me
i don't want to go
anywhere, do anything, give any
answers. the children are
vultures, the doorbell
a knell.
today
they're calling me, calling me
raising my spirit till
i must come back and be
here for them but am
alive as a ghost miles away, feeling you still
in me as if my need
could move my need.

THE SHEET

undecorative
my candor,
can't wrap you up,
if it can't come near you.

       being blank as a sheet
       can't hurt you

if i call you
my life, don't fail to hear me.
i have believed this sheet
across that city of dead
thought
and my need.

       could pull you

       between your head

       the flat shade
       flaps at the window, then bangs up.
       behind it, these wrapped bones wait
       which want you

      hard, resisting me

       lost
as you do. we are dressed   in each other's skulls
in our hardness as in
each other   when i haunt your bed.

THE YETI ARGUES ITS CASE

snowbound and sunblind in these blank
shifting dunes, you have put on your will like snowshoes
to rescue the heroine, and now you see
my blurred footprints and run.

the heroine is not here, you have saved her already
and you must stand.

you want me to vanish into the glare like a folktale.
i am no legend, i am the one you have rescued.
this was the task you were trained for. i give you this
plain as speech

if you wanted to be the hero who saved me
from these rough tracks i make, know
you are that hero in spite of all
your flight into abstracts. if you wanted
to carry me fire or pain
or any treasure so sharp
i could leap to you out of this matted coat,
shouting: at last, no shield from the cold, i am
no more than a flayed
animal now,

                    yes,
my friend, you may know
you do that.
                    if you wanted
one answer
from the heart of unanswering death
even where it mumbles in you, insisting
in public, before the demand
mountains of charts, tallies of whitespace,

hordes of reporters who greet the returning explorer
make of you
                    not to be heard

look up   /   hear
how
      shambling along the sheer edge of my nerves
through your windswept silences i am
that answer.

CLEARING DEBTS

                        a gong
over a stadium

twenty years ago
you spoke and made me
someone new to shout
at your door. i didn't know
my own voice anymore. five
years ago i tried
to clear that debt and failed,
my voice not charged enough
to shake you. now
your voice clamors in me
twenty years of built
resonance, tones i don't
know how to score, but let

ring changes. can you hear
from that hollow space where
no love nor hope
of love had been, what call
to battle rocks the stadium?

if this was yours
i echo and clangor and roar
it back into your ear.

THE ACCOUNTING

i tell you
as plain as i can, i have loved more
in the skills i brought to that task
(which were, don't kid yourself,
considerable) than i like to admit
to myself, who thought i made it happen
always out of fear
of the distance in me

but now see
that it is what you
who are closed to me
made   /   open.

HIGHWIRE

what can i bring you
that won't fall
like information? just this then /
if one could make me let go
my mind to pain, you are that one.

> when i'm a hundred years old
> and dead beside
> i'll have made everyone with eyes
> walk this wire with me.

we don't have to make
tensions, they make us
i might make
more of you if the truth were
a line i walked on to get there
obscuring itself as i went. i've
tried to be true to the fact
of a channel here. the balance
is use.

> i have to use you
> to pull words out
> of our love and string them tight
> the final outrage
> of grace.

THE HOUSEGUEST

i've thrown out
cut up, redone
so many selves, even though
i'm a saver, strings, rubberbands, screws,
one baked potato, three shrimp, i know i can make
something of them
                    burnt up
so many voices, what does it matter
if i burn this too.

                    poorhouse humility
                    so foreign to me i don't know
                    how to get rid of it now
                    it's walked in uninvited. see
                    it's the guest i won't ask to stay
                    for dinner, and now it wants
                    those potatoes, those bits of string,
                    those paperclips, won't wait for
                    the assurance of being wanted, lets go of that,
                                                                    quick

                    look, it will give you instead,
                    as its housegift, for the sunset
                    times, what you may not ever want, what
                    with candlelight, with the best of the vintage wine
                    we'd saved for somebody else
                    you certainly won't give me
this without
flattery or evasion   like a tall candle in you
the certainty you are
                    the center
                        of need.

SQUAWK

love breaks out of me
most when you won't
catch it and put it back / so
quickly i can't keep up. by the time
i rush to pick up
what i've said, it's far
away, won't let me get back there.

that parakeet in his cage talks
to his pretty blue mirror self the way
i talk to you, a horrible
fury of lust and the joy of lust
gobbling up his voice, yes,
and sometimes what i love best
(though to him love's equal) tenderness
tearing his voice away

                    i say
happy to be
what he is
not knowing what he should be.

STRAIGHT FROM
THE STEREO SET

the old plaintive yammer
i won't turn off yells
from a dozen speakers at once
in all the rooms, I, I,
in a miserable shrill
whine i dare call joy

don't tell me what you
want to hear is the I
in my voice. be very sure
every line grooved into this disk
what we have to hear or
die is You. where
are You.

whatever i make to deny
i have not kept still, and this
constant, uneasy flow
round go round and go round
of energy is my joy
even though i say so.

ONE DAY THE DOORBELL

you're in conference, saving Hungarians,
buried, deaf, you're
not here, not so much, no, but
one day the doorbell,
striped eagles flapping their wings, rocketing
care packages down (and i need them), they're
mined, they go off,
flash, sputter, burn out, but one
i grab, quick, yank out the fuse, throw it
away (across the hall the old lady's
door burns down but I don't care),
i grab, quick, tear, in it a record

                                        (your voice,
                        so low where i drowned it i have to
                        guess what it seems to say)

so i put it on, turn out
the light, forgot to turn on
the sound, god damn it, frantic
crazy bitch in heat, i dive
onto it, drool all over it, crunch, gobble
it down, ouch, the cut edges cut
my throat, my blood is choking me, i don't care,
i've got to hear

                                        (scratchy
                        voice under the voice:
                        i hear you, i'm
                        slow to answer but
                        never fear, i'll get there

some fine international
rescue committee you are
don't you know

records never hear
anyone, they just fill
silence

HOW TO DO IT

i want to come
with a dream of you
and won't let
myself do it, though
the dream is responsive, how
long can i hold out

you can hear how
i've kept no subterfuge,
no cleverness, no wit
no self to hide me, no image
only the naked voice.

techniques i know
i say that without shame
to make my guts on a string
dance prettily for you, draw
plans of the kingdom / how
to take me, how i plan
to take you.

                    i can't use them.
let me tell you
now, with an unsure voice
diffidence, a mumble. please
choose to hear.

THE CAREFUL HOUSES

these careful houses
i keep with neat
each in its place the act
of breaking nothing, of minding
the details, of trying half truths
to spare
        you
            pain
these walls love's usage makes:

        if i could be
        implacable, if i could
        require that same careless, hard
        truthfulness of myself
        that i love in you

what would the houses say
in their carefulness
        do they want me to shout
at the bar, in the Opera House, loud
till the glasses crack?

          i don't
        want to scare you
        i wish i could keep you
        i want to touch you
        so much.

THE PROMISE

it is finite
the rain, don't worry,
it can't go on forever

i should try to put back
the craziness in me   that clear beam
which let me stay   sunlight
                        to walk on
sure that our bones remember
the ease, the balances
of dancing / soon as i set words down

                        forgive me
                        it will come down anyway
i fall   rain curtain
when i write
my life over   each drop
                        covers the last
erasing you
washing me out   the temptation
                        to make a good thing better
                        and lose it.

THE LIGHTING FIXTURE

floats

an ornate error over us but can't call
me back from the lovecoast
we travel now.

stubborn, i make
out of memory not love but the raw
materials thereof.

IN REGRET

how shall i tell you
what careless of all but happiness i have omitted
to say so many times /

                    how good
has been the line down your back to my hands, how right
your throat has felt
to my lips. that spot of sweat
your head, wet, has printed
year after year on my breast as you slept

                    and my back got
                    stiff /
                         i didn't dare move
and moved and broke
everything.

THE TRUE STORY

i've tried to make it
too many ways, naked,
over the Falls in a barrel,
on Main Street, the Via Veneto
tucked cozily under my elbow,
fireworks and atomic
energy gilding my hair, or
strut my Dior mind
in its sequins over the footlights.

nothing would do the trick.
i have only the joy
you are.

VOYAGER

dearest, i have been
where the sun shown
days on end
and not known
where i was

        lain
lilac strewn
under the moss
line of earth

           seen
my eyes turn
stone
in that moving
again

i know a thousand ways
to hold and not let go
a thousand dreams
that show the way to sleep

                  can lead
you where you want to be
i know love
from the inside
of my
      dark
          molding
              womb

and i can take
you home
if you will lie
down

Six

How the Dead Count

ON THE PORCH OF THE TRAVELERS' REST

Sint Maarten

"Holiday, holiday, on the very first day of the year . . . ."
—Ballad of Little Matthy Grove and Lord Barnard's Wife

on the porch of our inn, where you and i, both diners, celebrate
holiday, holiday, and the year spins into its wellspring,
hang three charms for the wind, two glass birds and a plate-
copper fish which the seabreeze turns with the year to make sing.

vacationers will come here to celebrate the rite
of breaking bread together / we shall laugh and take life
from what silence lies spiced, garnished on our plate
as the hummingbird nests on this porch through day and night.

this trembling, hovering bird has built her house over our heads
on the copper fish / in the midst of our friendly chatter floats quiet
                                                    | as day,
and i see her begin weeks ago to weave her bed
where our hulks will cross, sailing the currents round her like moons
                                                    | that wait out her joy.

such tides have carried her to nesting time
as have carried us to love and to this inn
but her tides have taught her what mud to use, what twigs to find
and in what fine pattern and ordered moves weave her nest, mine no
                                                    | such thing.

i, creature of my blood and knowing how it flows,
read no clear design in my entrails that can tell
what way to turn, or when i must let love go
where it will, even to die, as i circle our lives from above like a
                                                    | great angry owl in search of its kill.

alone and unknowing in the waltzing sea sprinkled with stars
                                                    | i spun into song with you
alone on her swaying nest the hummingbird floats and breathes
balanced on her copper fish where she chose to go
far from all safer places where she might nest and breed.

99

that bird in her ignorance knows what she should do
as the moon swings its silence into the stars' cold stream.
alone in the echoing current only moons sail through
she stirs constantly in ways too little to see, and sings in a voice no
|hungry woman or man can hear:

great emptiness great sand and heartbeat day
i hovered the raving day and the sanded foam drilled holes in me
something i heard of silence, some specks tasted of salt spray,
touched a frothing of loose jelly spawned in the quickening sea

there are ways of seeing i know that pull me to sympathy
with those moons like eyes that move the world from a world a world away
ways of moving i keep that slide in and out with the sea
heaped-up poems of lives that sweep in lazily from across the bay.

i am caught up in the world's blood and i flow with it
what seem to be my rhythms sway with the circling tides
outside my veins. i wake and my sunlight splits
your day. i dream and the horned owl hooting rides

your moon away. he sweeps the night for minute prey.
if i, hummingbird, leave my nest he will have me for sweet
at the close of a mess of dreams / if my mate come to me now
bearing nectar or ant in his beak, the owl will take him for condiment.

sweet meal, fine meal i taste with this grinding death of my mate, with
|the air and the sea salt
driven into my breast feathers with every wind's harbinger's gust
and i tell my unknown chicks i will leave them as soon as i may / i have felt
love swell me and carry and drop me / i shall praise in each feather's turn
|the turning to love's death and the world's rest.

THE LIVES OF RAIN

your life has been on my hands like a dead fish
turned so quickly you wouldn't have wanted to scale
or eat it, glow worm fingers that won't stay silent
under the pocked rain. it is your hands now
that lie on my hands. poor fish,
they have nothing to tell me, can't know or move in air.
without moving you give them to me with all their life.
now it is my hands that lie on my hands,
my hands have become a burden, heavy, wet,
my life lies on them, the life in them lies on them,
they stay heavy, stiff, frozen in rigor mortis,
bent sideways, tailfins up, they died flapping
and will not signal you. they will not tell you
of any life under water, any green in the sea.
they will weigh on themselves until the currents turn them
to little flecks of algae, fishdung and scum.

THREE POWER DANCES

First Dance: God Who Walks Like A Bear

a great Female Bear
     wide as a house   sings
out of Her dark cave
     under Her fringed roots   sings
     up from Her furred clutch   sings
     that hides the mouth of Her hunger   sings
out of Her sounding womb hung
     with vines warming the honey   sings

          sweetheart let Me grieve you
               with a new music
        made of old men's bones
                    loosen your tongue
                    loosen your blood with music
        too stiff to move with Me
                    walk you from note to note
        thick at the joints with knobs
                    bang our sweet bones together

          sweetheart let Me empty you
               hollow you out with moving
        cric crac cric crac
        I am too old to dance with you
        but I will dance you a pretty dance
        cric crac

          sweetheart let Me skin you
               with rhythms of My furred touch
        My great hairy shapeless hands
               so soft you'll never feel
                    through brush of My drums

        how the layers slide off you

to lay you bare to love
while every stripped muscle cries

let the old She Bear lie
down and hold you in Her arms.

Second Dance: The Bear Dancer's Stomp

woke from Her hungry sleep
   all the winter moons long
     rumbling with it, felt
         the earth bleed away from Her /
         Her man in his new pride
         pace out rockfall and wood,
         measure Her space,

                           stomped
I'll come away My lovely man
   to stamp with you, to shake with you
   My great, shambling animal dance
       that changes the hunting moon,
       holds back the day

see Me take up My Powers here
        Mask, Staff and Bear Dress,
hear the night ride Me

I'll walk you first a blear Bear
   shaggy at elbow
   heavy the broad back wide as your Mother's house
   old Woman of the mountain, massive and black lipped
   to squat in My door

is it war here, My lovely / you turn your mask loose on Mine?
look how I take your dress
   crow you a Rooster Bear heavy with feathers
   strut high My curved spurs, shake wattles, shake tail,

Bear painted with dawn stripes,
   clawed Singer of morning Who crows up the Sun

I'll snort you a Stallion, flare wide My nose holes,
   take from you mean snout,
   Bear rearing and screaming to strike with My hooves
                                                        hard
   hammer your skull, split the cup, spill the brain

see Me snap now, the swamp God, Bear edged with scissor
                                                        teeth,
      whip with My ridged tail, My lizardly loves churn,
      Bear grown all Alligator, Bear of the swamp heart
      snip you right through the trunk
      slice the heart's tree

shrill with My sharp beak I've circled above you
see how I fly you blind / Bear with an Eagle's wings
      Bear with My wingspan that measures the edge of sight,
      beak missiles home to nest deep in your eyes
home to My call letters hear how I mark my scent
      rat-tat on the dust skin; *be:* pound you flat; *be:* dance you
                                                        down;
      be: My spurs to strike such music up, *be* your teeth to
                                                        jingle
                           at My waist /
      your head *be* My hooves' bell
      your heart *be* My steel drum

hair, scales, hooves, wattles, furred beak, ridged tail
      these have I torn from you
      with these I hold back your day,
      your death dance, your night of war
this *is* My Power dance
this *is* My Bear stomp
this My bones sail and ride

as I plummet   /   to lie like you
bound in My hide.

Third Dance: The Last Bear's Going

you have made the world unfit for me
your air not my air
the day comes down indifferently
the night brings a changed taste
the sour juice your veins make
shrivels my tongue

gently the moon down
    the hills down the long down
        leaves of the world's fall
           glides down to sleep
the snow down deep
drift bellied winter out

not to be mine again

cold and as i go
naked in your human night
my skin dress my coarse hair
covers the bones i wear

i die
        into your moon
i slide
        into your blood
i ride
        the spilled night out
here where my salt rough sea tongue works
        through caverns of your mouth
        slow

Master of Earth
    how thick
    flows

        this Your life
that chokes me
    Your long night down.

MORNING LIGHT

for Marilyn Hacker

this is a place
where people live
you will not find anything neat here
that is not a hat on the hatrack
that is not a man's shape on the chair

this is a place
where the dead stays real
and alive all day in its room
it cracks its knuckles over its breakfast tray
rocking, rocking, while it waits for the door to open
out of its skull

this is a place
where the woman sits
all day on the edge of the stove
waiting for something to take fire

that is not last year's news she shreds with the cheese
that is not next year's bloodbank of fashion
in the rag she burns
with the toast on her back in the morning light
that tells her
she's too old.

SHARES

(for Nancy and Bill Beaver and their children)

morning: the last winter day's sun glints
    on the cold glass buildings' scales in rows
        i am not a city fish
i think, as this march wind flings
    dust into my nose
      not made to swim
or thrive in the fuming tail spawn
    of buses, or hold
    my own in an undertow
      of cars, and my mind shifts

to a tawny and green world
    where the air and i lay
with you in the belly of the earth and tilled the sun
till it bloomed in our skin
    and its dust motes
sang scales on the steel fish sides
    of the sliding air. all day
we timed the tides coming in
by the clock of our heart vein /
    sometimes felt one huge wave
with a flood or a fall, low lull-off or all roar
    take more than its share
    of time as it overcame
its spent backsliding brother combing down the shore
sometimes the weeds floated
motionless all startime
    silence long, and i thought:
      i would say
what the cockles say
    lifted up in that great breath
of sea and then expelled
    on the rocks to break open or hold
      what the small shells
      of the sea snails and the heart cells

of our green tides play
in the proud brass roar
        of their lives,
                or sing in their slick
                whirl, spinning towards silence on the bent shore line
lives' end

                cast up in New York
the buses roar through avenues of my blood
like schooled whales, the dust whirls
in the pools of wind like small shelled
spinning shrimp, shards of litter hum
        along the strand of the curb like
little crabs coming
alive in the tides we draw
        after us
                see
        it is all one
                and foaming

Spring leaps out
of the shark mouths of the cars
where the holiday families
        man woman and hungry
                animal eddying down
to the country for shark's play
break surface and shout
        like teeth into the sun

            we will have our share of day.

EARTHS

for Robert Clayton Casto

my friends are earths for me to ruffle and toss
all tumble and roar and hunger / they feel my voice
before they hear me, grains of sand, drillbits that sting

murmur of air so enduring no one will hear
whistled erosion devouring the inner ear.
they are not pretty, the songs i have to sing.

and though i go on in a voice too constant to hear
they know my voice / though my breath eats up their soil
they listen, they run to my yammering, follow on call.

my friends are what holds me when i run to earth.

INVITATION TO THE VOYAGE

(an epithalamium for Carolyn Kizer and John Woodbridge—April 11, 1975)

we are out looking for joy tonight, coursing the stars
like last year's raggedy pack of hounds, having been earthbound all
                                                            | year
in our cold hearth-sullenness, turning around ourselves
without turning anything up, picking up the last lick
of a meteor's trail to set us right, and we've found no course to steer
this sun round again but the old maps, no chart to build our cities right
but the old deathshead that rhymes our blood. we've turned into our
selves until we've become the ark(c)'s last tailspin
problem in navigation that no star solves.

i thought to set this lovers' world on its track again
                                as is the time writ way
of poets, and forgot all such minute, vainglorious ends
when i saw these two lovers rise to give and take hands
across our distances. best voyagers of joy
let me give you this gift which my puritan soul must fear
not good enough since it was made, not slowly over your years
of brilliance with one hundred gravities' weight
                                pulling its mass awry
                                but easily as you hold hands
across the moon's face tonight, quickly as a rocket lifts
the world away and nakedly, without veils, leaps through the
                                                    | airless
                                                        black
                                                            and full
diffidence of space to the nearest thought.

astronomers of our passion hurtling through the sky
long seasons fixed in love between one star and the next
what voyage can we invite you to; you have invited us
on the voyage of lovers' nights where through generations in space
you shall be the double star of our bearings, the beacon we harbor near

to heat our minds that watch you all the fireball
passage and ardor of your celestial flight.

now in the mapped stars' turning you give birth to yourselves:
you, Carolyn, have built poems spacious as worlds
in all parts of the world, turned the common arch of our speech
to the great gate of a cathedral in which our lives run to worship,
and now scan that most resonant poem, a good man's love;
you, John, have planned the towers of man's soul in a grid of parking
                                               |lots,
have plotted cities out of the nightmare star
our plague-dealing hearts have blasted, made from dead hands
                                           | lifeworks,
to find that towering edifice, that blueprint of joy, a woman's mind
                                            |that lives
in challenge and in ambitious work. no random play of electric
                            sparks, but a white flowering
                                     | rose
                    window of light, set
in your heavy glow like suns
you shall warm our lives with your giants' heat of love.
together you shall weave streets jeweled with song
in which will rise theatres of noble stance where all our poet's
                                |work may fare
as forests to stand up and flight their hearts into our mouths all
                                |speechquake long
and tell how in the city of the mind the poet's heart must reign.

i have looked in grief at the suffering of my friends,
in awe of their great hearts, and how they ceaselessly sail
tides, orbits of the expanding universe of night in us, and glow
                            |and hold up bloody hands
torn by the meteored reefs they rake. without fail
that lightyears' wrack is ended. we will have galaxies that sing in our
                                | globe's eyes
we will have joys that crow in candlelight
under the shuttered eaves of dreams. beyond all fall of cities
we will have you, love's architects and poets,

our pleasure to track through the milky way all summer through
and into winter when we burn with a crystal flame
to follow. we have seen you rise and flourish, and have known
in you what love is; now you shall sing
in our minds' blood our true fame which is your own.

TWO DREAM SONGS AND A SONNET

for Mr. B——

First Song

famous Henry and loved once found himself
pictured in gold frames on the rims of eyes
under the shale shades of this continent
deep bedded. for all he gib regret
to his many admirers, Mr. Bones,
dese bones am not content.

do you speak of a crazy man, Mr. Bones?—I does.
and was he hurt in his words and of good grace
not made purveyor?—to our long joy he was
well damaged.
       what of his life save can we but by praise?
—why, Mr. Bones, let him pass
and toss with his river at ease.

Sonnet

the world's great novels hung for Berryman's ears
like tasseled pendants that he'd thought to light.
something that world required in fireburst tears
his mind burned to let fall to it that cool night.
"I thought some things too long and thought them ill /
prepared am I for holding, while this hurld
tinpot cannonball makes its score of me, still. what fill
I've had call mine and sieve me out of the world."
what was there for the night to empty of
so cleanly that his whistle stumbled wet
in the eaves, or what fine turnout meant for love
left had been, he no inkling of could get,
nor answer that question well phrased: "whaffor?"
caught in the not unmentionable war.

Second Song

on a sudden the shape forever of words began
Berryman to change, savvy, tickle and weight
made other, so that we speak him now. in de slambanging noon
Henry waffled and were grave. later, to be wif all dem greats,
himself flung down, of de rivers rushing one,
our Berryman did, so bravely under de moon.

wise Berryman, that did much your sly mind wrench
and huff in waters breaking   to be in a woman's skin
wild with that bloody show,
do not of this birth make such prodigious work:
bear, poet, my fine, dead, down   slow
                                        slow
só, friend, it will come.

HAPPY JACK COMES HOME

such jolly nights, my old friend, Jack Hammer, since last i talked with
|you
in your rattling hole of the heart under the Colorado reefs
where the sharks wear human faces and their teeth go click click

i have not bitten anything out of the rocks i could take home and keep
nothing that lights up, nothing that starts wires humming, makes
|needles
dance, nothing to wrap with a ribbon and give to Mother

oh it is quiet here. what quiet you have brought in the wake
of your bustle and slamming. not a mouth stirs in the kitchen
where we cook up sharks' fin soup and wait for the shark to fall in

yet the sun will rise up with rage and burst with rage
out of the soup kettle we are stirring, you and i,
and envy,
why, envy will hammer in our veins like the pulse of a maniac

stuttering. there will be bombs planted in every locker room
where the human soup is stirred and stirred and tasted.
the boys of summer will fall like the summer flies

legs pulled off by that curious chef of luminosity
who wants to see what we taste like without our wills
to move us. our legs will not get us out of here.

we will lie silently in the soup, heavy as fizzing rocks that throb
when you touch them, we will lie silently in the morgue
in green plastic bags, and be whirled around the sun where no

history tells of our progress into a safe
burning
rest,

and the stuttering of needle on graph paper registers a mindless
                                                  |holding pattern.
the death of the brain is all it takes for this transplant. they will
                                                  |take out your brain

and use it to make history sing in the silent book of our deaths.

YOU HAVE SEEN THE WOLF'S RIDE

("You have seen the wolf's ride and that comes ever before great tidings . . ."
—*Njal's Saga*, tr. by E. R. Eddison in *The Worm Ouroboros*)

what would you do
    if a wolf walked through
        the sunlit patches on West Eighty-seventh Street,

showed his teeth at the traffic light
    on the corner, snapped at bumpers and hems of skirts,
        chased my three girls on their bikes, and pulled them down?

in all small thoroughfares
    and crossings the wolf bares
        his teeth

in tangles and wrangling of
    my delicate children
        at play

in niches of the long passage
    my grandmother took
        to die.

i look back
    on the gentle poor who must crack
        my bones to stay quick

those poor who came
    like my grandmother and were taught
        to leave the old savage game

home at the crossroads.
    i look back
        past her day and her crossing

to the cold patched sunlight
    on the keep floor, and Count Vlad's
        cry, exultant:

hear them
     the wolves
          of my country

howling
     for blood. children,
          you have seen the wolf's ride

blaze with sirens out
     from faultlines, ingles, its switchblades unfurled
          on the bloodwet flags of my city,

seen the track that flaming brand
     seared through your hands
          which caught

the triumph,
     the yammer,
          the pack

after the lead wolf
     in full cry gathered
          to harry

while the last of us sit
     by the signal light, watching the sun
          go down that throat.

HOW THE DEAD COUNT

for Andrew Goodman, James Chaney, Michael Schwerner

I

i count the waste
                    (let me keep you awhile / here
of these dead on ground
                    (let me measure you
                              common and sweet
              to praise (make a casket for you
              to fly these dead in their holy foam and scum
                              honey and wine
              to the crab nebula, to the jewels of orion's belt
              where they may lie /
                              clean
in battle stations whose lives fired for an end
the strongest of those they hoped to serve
                              now scorn

shades of the great revolutionaries
                    a hundred years from now
spin around spin around the dust cloud
                    that was our town
their teeth shine in the dark
              their beards and nails grow long
              their nostrils flare

                              have a care
                              sweet singer
                              look for me
                                   in all
                              the changing air
                              and circles of the will
sniff the air for green
                    rake dust from the dust for proud
test all standing pools for pure
                    comb through the sun's torn hair

for shine
                those worlds are gone   and in the earth
                nobody lives there   when it must rise
                                               swollen against all will
                                               like a gorge rise
                                               swollen with proud men
                                               in the root and rut of heat
                                               lumpish, heavy with greed
                                               that outlives the last green stand
                                                       oh in the sweet
                                               and foul and changing air
                                               look for me
                                               i'll be there

Karl Marx whose capital will you count
                                    and burn
Bakunin what's found to bomb
                                    generations
grown old in sour dismay
and excess of will to move, prophets grown cold
in excess of passion to burn
Nineveh, burn Tyre
theorists grown hard
with plotting the Dow Jones plunge and spill of hands
you, wise / you, weary / you, furious / you, frustrate
tellers of the world's ill
ends   /   bend
down from your high, indifferent
all consuming fire
trail orbits of the fallout mind
                         pity the young

                                    see
                         how the dead count, the young,
                         cobalted, heavy water space
                         ship and radium cratered faces count, see
                         how the dead count who died
                         in just or unjust war
                         young, pity the young

3

Goodman, Chaney, Schwerner:
(oh yes this grass
green grows on you
in solitude between teeth
sunning the porches of your stair) what can you make
of peace or peaceful exercise
of choice / where you toss
here / under the house / in tides beyond choice
shall it be broadcast
of you in every pulsar
and common market square where scholars dole
the praise, the blame, be published in Askelon,
in the streets, on the fall graphed tiles of Askelon:

what history could tell they would not heed
what theory could plan they slipped around
what rhetoric could hold they stepped outside
what innocence could shield they spilled away
and cast upon the common ground, and died.

the lilac and the yew
purple and swell in you
fools, dreamers popping up like clowns
   on springs out of the burnt
      openings under the powdered stair
         flesh falling off in strings
            mouths hanging loose at last
               knees spread, each corpse astride
                  the shoulders of the last
                     piled behind closet doors
                       paneled in walls, stoned,
                          bricked up, packed in, stamped down
                          in just or unjust war
                          and nothing done for good
back from the grave at each day's end to tell me
how with your checkpoint grins
you put on my lips
   you put on my hair

you speak, your mouths suck in my air
    you hold / tight, you're sure
              how with each crosshatching vine
              that climbs, that rots to you
              twines the bones,
                    ankle to brain
                        up through the eyeholes
              man after man, you can will
              me or some voice in me
              to live / breathe / be
              the promise made / and died for
              man after man, no end
          tell us, shall the quasars broadcast
          in Nineveh, Askelon:
          as you dream you shall be dreamt, my friends?

so should i say
shooting the bloodcount light
      rapids of common day
green life of the dead and fresh
red seedberries of decay

                  is it not time
                  to breathe and find an end
spinning around
          Ché where will you stay

4

the ghosts of a hundred worlds are whirling
                    mad priests in a daze
                    fresh from a hundred years away
                    in the ice age that keeps them sane
they do not know the time of day
they do not know what names they owned
they do not know how old they are
                    and dry
who died young
                    they will not tell the taste of rain
                    or spring desire
or how
            green rots the tongue
or when
            you can see through / them

                                oh and in what sunlight
                                and in what rage
                                and in what love and joy
                                the fire will come
                                as it has done
                                shining through opened cheeks
                                gas, slime of the stars / swirl of the
                                                    planets' hair
                                through silver muscled walled
                                orbits without hope

perpetually dumb
who died young
            died young

waste i celebrate
and waste i praise
the eaten dead who rise
to fall and fall to rise

wide doors open
tell us now
thou, selfless, possessed, worker in the cellarage
from what stiff box you crawled
fingers over the rim and the lid
raised half seas over ivy
creep climb rocking to finger drink
up MissLiberty
and what ship's hold creaks
as you pick off one by one captain mate purser
and rise to eat again

they swear they mean to have you
                                even
as you are
            they swear they know a way
to work some change in you
                    whether in teeth or hair
                    to make your body grow
                    into some climbing thing
and unforeseen
            they swear they've come to stay
men without bones or voice
touch by touch risen from the box
we stowed those dead selves in   to sway
                                as we do now, dumb
                                sea anemone maws, red
                                umbrella polyps, tide washed
                                        groundcover slime
                                in the morse code spotted zero
                                hour pulse of the countdown night

where innocence in its charged
                          hurtling
current
          and starféd stream
green / grows on you
in what ship's hold you choose

6

                    out of this whirlpool of tills that dumbly tenders
                                                              you
                    i will say: sweet are the bells
                    out of the earth of spills in the wet boles' mouths
                    of the sea beasts, the flowers
                    out of this black hole, this throat in space
                    the gaseous bells in the sky and under my feet
                    the bells of grapes i tread down to bloody wine, the
                                                              tongues,
                                        the soft tongues
              which mindlessly clabber:
nothing will change us
no debt will be wiped out / no account settled
because of what we do / hear us jangle
our jungle climes, our ice ages, one on another
transparent as our words, we are / you

                    current as coins
                    of tongues, current as honey
                    current as magnets alive, sweet as coins ringing
                    the changes, sweet the voices
                    of the bells, the dolorous bells, the sonorous gongs,
                    the ponderous gongs, the living, breathing bells
                    of the blood of the dead, the dead
                    of the mouths of my city

                    the great bell souls that shift
                    and sway into the heart
                    of day, that swell open, as flowers of sails do

as flowers of worlds
as bodies do, rent, streaming to the light, as mouths, as longhaired
                                                            mouths,
comets hot for meat they never touched, as black mouths
in space, hot for bodies they never tongued, never swallowed, as the
                                                    dead count
        their wounds and number them continually
        as the wind numbers the leaves it mouths, as the
                                    wind out of space
        numbers the loves we lose, as the wind mumbles
        the minds we leave, as the number of the arc
        numbers our lives

                            oh in what air and in what earth
                            what airt of light
                            shall we climb and fill
                            our billfold flowering mouths
                            with marrow of you, as the dead
                                                    count
                            as the dead count their words, as
                                            the dead count
                            their wounds, as the dead count
                            their lives in us, as the dead count
                            continually, sweet singer say and
                                                        say
                            as the dead count.

Note: airt is an early English word that means both earth and air (basically, the planet
and its atmosphere).

THE LIFT-OFF OF AN ABSENCE

we were not so far from home
that it could be added up. i wanted to leave you
with some idea of the furnace room when i sent
my mind up, showering sparks down through the concrete floor
and burning a redrimmed crater
eyesocket west of the reservoir. i wanted to drop
with the fallout some flickering glimpse,
from the corners of your eyes, which insisted on leaving,
of the janitor's work gloves
crossed on the battered chair
with the lining ripped to show the great cloud
in Andromeda, and one coiled spring poking up
lightyears your side of darkness, the overalls hanging
in freefall on the chords of Berenice's Hair
while the sweat dried off and the black oil stains set.

under the steel ribs
of the elevator shaft the pump knocks in the walls.
you are not here but somewhere else. you were
here when i was not somewhere else.
we will be together in the great cloud
in Andromeda tomorrow night when the furnace lifts off
to join us. i can see the stars through every crack in your ribs
as your teeth burn cratered white holes in space
exploding the pulsar sun

                         your mind which i have loved
will seed the stars. we have not been far from here
and we are at home.